in a cabin
in a wood

ADAPTED BY
Darcie McNally

ILLUSTRATED BY
Robin Michal Koontz

COBBLEHILL/DUTTON · NEW YORK

For Kaitlyn, Justin, Denny, and my friends from
Camp Cleawox (especially Tajar)—DMcN

For Linda Brodie and all her critters—RMK

Library of Congress Cataloging-in-Publication Data
McNally, Darcie.   In a cabin in a wood /
adapted by Darcie McNally ; illustrated by Robin Michal Koontz.
p.   cm.
Summary: An adaptation of the familiar song in which
animals in the woods beg for shelter from the hunter.
ISBN 0-525-65035-0
1. Children's songs—United States—Texts.   [1. Animals—Fiction.
2. Songs.]   I. Koontz, Robin Michal, ill.   II. Title.
PZ8.3.M4599In   1991
782.42164'0268—dc20   89-25192
CIP   AC

Published in the United States by Cobblehill Books,
an affiliate of Dutton Children's Books,
a division of Penguin Books USA Inc.

Typography by Kathleen Westray
Printed in Hong Kong
First edition   10 9 8 7 6 5 4 3

In a cabin in a wood,
little man by the window stood.
Saw a rabbit hopping by,
knocking at the door.
"Help me, help me, help!" it said.
"Before the hunter shoots me dead."

"Come, little rabbit, come inside.
Safely you'll abide."

In a cabin in a wood,
little man by the window stood.
Saw a possum waddling by,
knocking at the door.
"Help me, help me, help!" it wailed.
"Before the hunter pulls my tail."

"Come, little possum, come inside.
Safely you'll abide."

In a cabin in a wood,
little man by the window stood.
Saw a raccoon prancing by,
knocking at the door.
"Help me, help me, help!" it begged.
"Before the hunter thumps my leg."

"Come, little raccoon,
come inside.
Safely you'll abide."

In a cabin in a wood,
little man by the window stood.
Saw a beaver dashing by,
knocking at the door.
"Help me, help me, help!" it purred.
"Before the hunter grabs my fur."

"Come, little beaver,
come inside.
Safely you'll abide."

In a cabin in a wood,
little man by the window stood.
Saw a moose come thudding by,
knocking at the door.
"Help me, help me, help!" it cried.
"Before the hunter whacks my hide."

"Come, little moose, come inside.
Safely you'll abide."

In a cabin in a wood,
little man by the window stood.
Saw a skunk come hopping by,
knocking at the door.
"Help me, help me, help!" it said.
"Before the hunter shoots me dead."

"Come, little skunk,
come inside.

Safely you'll abide."

in a cabin in a wood

First verse traditional; other verses by Darcie McNally

In a ca-bin in a wood, lit-tle man by the win-dow stood.

Saw a rab-bit hop-ping by, knock-ing at the door.

"Help me! Help me! Help!" it said. "Before the hun-ter shoots me dead!"

"Come little rab-bit come in-side, safe-ly you'll a - bide."

SONG PLAY ACTIONS

Form a roof with
your hands.

Hold pretend binoculars
up to your eyes.

Use two fingers in a "V"
and hop them along.
*(Make up your own motions
for the other animals!)*

Pretend you are knocking
at the cabin door.

Throw your hands up into
the air and look scared.

Cover face with your hands
and shiver with fear.

Motion for the animal to
come inside with you.

Pretend you are gently
petting the animal.

Music reproduced from WEE SING, published by Price Stern Sloan, Inc.,
Los Angeles, California. Copyright © 1977, 1979 by Pamela Beall and Susan Nipp.